Rat-a-tat-tat

Written by Michaela Morgan

Illustrated by Dave Williams

Collins

Rat-a-tat-tat! Who is that?
Open the door and see.

Rat-a-tat-tat

WELCOME

3

It's a cat in a yellow hat, and she wants to play with me.

Rat-a-tat-tat! Who is that?
Open the door and see.

Rat-a-tat-tat

It's a fox in blue and
white socks.

Come in and play with me.

Rat-a-tat-tat! Who is that?
Open the door and see.

It's a goat in a coat ...

... a dog and a frog ...

... and a bear in pyjamas eating bananas.

They **all** want to play
with me.

Rat-a-tat-tat! Who is that?
Open the door and see.

11

It's a dinosaur.
ROAR!

You can't play with me!

Who is at the door?

1

2

4

5

15

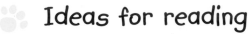

Ideas for reading

Written by Clare Dowdall, PhD
Lecturer and Primary Literacy Consultant

Learning objectives: draw on grammatical awareness, to read with expression and intonation; use a range of cues to work out unfamiliar words; blend phonemes to read CVC words in rhyming and non-rhyming sets; read on sight high frequency words; explore familiar themes through improvisation and role play.

Curriculum links: Music: exploring sounds, including chants

High frequency words: who, that, wants, with, is, the, and, see, a, in, she, dog, cat, all, you

Interest words: open, door, yellow, blue, white, socks, goat, coat, frog, bear, pyjamas, bananas, dinosaur, roar

Word count: 98

Resources: whiteboard

Getting started

- Look at the front and back covers together. Read the title and blurb and ask the children to predict why the cat is knocking at the door.

- Look at pp2–3. Practise reading *Rat-a-tat-tat! Who is that?* with expression. Emphasise the rhythm and rhyme of the sentences.

- Look carefully at the picture and ask the children to identify Mum and the child. Ask who may be behind the door. Turn the page and read together *It's a cat in a yellow hat, and she wants to play with me.*

- Play a game in which children substitute the words cat and hat for other rhyming pairs, e.g. *it's a bat looking rather fat; it's a pig in a curly wig.* List the rhyming pairs on a whiteboard.

Reading and responding

- Ask the children to read together up to p13. Encourage the children to emphasise rhyming words and rhythm and to read with expression. Pause on each new spread so the children can predict who will arrive next and to discuss the story.

- Help the children to read unfamiliar words and phrases, emphasising the rhyme and the strategies they could use (e.g. using picture cues, initial sounds).